Silly Billy

Paul Stewart is the very funny, very talented author of more than twenty books for children, including *The Edge Chronicles*, a collaboration with Chris Riddell.

Chris Riddell is a well-known illustrator and political cartoonist. His work appears in the *Observer* and the *New Statesman*, and he has illustrated many picture books and novels for young readers.

Both live in Brighton, where they created the Blobheads together.

Titles in the Blobheads series

All Blobheads titles can be ordered at your local bookshop or are available by post from Book Service by Post (tel: 01624 675137).

The Blobheads

Silly Billy

Paul Stewart
and Chris Riddell

MACMILLAN
CHILDREN'S BOOKS

P.S. For Anna and Joseph
C.R. For Jack

First published 2000 by Macmillan Children's Books
a division of Macmillan Publishers Limited
25 Eccleston Place, London SW1W 9NF
Basingstoke and Oxford
www.macmillan.co.uk

Associated companies throughout the world

ISBN 0 330 38977 7

1 3 5 7 9 8 6 4 2

A CIP catalogue record for this book is available from
the British Library.

Typeset by SX Composing DTP, Rayleigh, Essex
Printed and bound in Great Britain by Mackays of Chatham plc, Kent

Chapter One

"And where do you think you're going, Billy?" said Mr Barnes as he caught sight of his older son hurrying past the open kitchen door. He pushed another spoonful of pumpkin and passion-fruit fool into baby Silas's mouth. "Billy?"

"Yummy-gummy," gurgled a very gooey Silas, happily spitting it out on to the floor.

Billy stopped and poked his head round the door. "Over to Simon's," he said. "He's got a new computer game. *Splat Attack 2.* And he promised I could have a go."

Mr Barnes looked up and frowned. "*Splat Attack?*" he said, dripping more of the glistening gloop on to Silas's head. "What's that all about?"

"It's really cool, Dad," said Billy. "You've got to save the earth from hordes of aliens hurling purple pies."

"Aliens hurling purple pies?" said Mr Barnes. "How ridiculous."

"Oh, I don't know," said Billy. "It's not as ridiculous as you might think!"

If his dad thought *they* were ridiculous, then he should see the three aliens who lived up in Billy's bedroom. Now they *were* ridiculous. They had arrived out of the blue – or rather, out of the toilet – in search of the High Emperor of the Universe who was, according to their so-called Great Computer, none other than Billy's baby brother, Silas.

Mr Barnes wiped Silas's head with a damp sponge. "Anyway," he said. "You're not playing any games this afternoon. You promised Mrs Turbot that you'd deliver those leaflets for the school fair."

"Oh, but—" Billy protested.

"And you still haven't washed Mr Arkwright's car, even though he gave you a pound last week to do it."

"Yes, but I—"

"And don't forget Mrs Ramsden's lawn. You promised to mow it for her ages ago."

Billy sighed.

"And before any of that, I want you to go and tidy your room," Mr Barnes continued, without taking a breath. "It's an absolute tip!"

"Oh, Da-ad," Billy complained.

"Now!" said Mr Barnes.

"Goo, goo, goo," Silas burbled contentedly as Billy stomped up the stairs.

Mr Barnes called up after him. "And don't slam your bedroom door—"

SLAM!

*

"I do wish you wouldn't bang the door like that," said the spotty red and purple rubber ring.

"Yes," said the striped red and purple beach ball irritably. "Why do you always have to be so loud?"

"You made me jump," complained the giant fluffy pink elephant.

"Oh, be quiet, the lot of you!" said Billy, flinging himself on the bed. "No

wonder my dad thinks the bedroom's messy, with you lot cluttering up the place in your ridiculous disguises," he said, eyeing the elephant furiously.

The rubber ring, the beach ball and the elephant morphed back into the three Blobheads: Kerek, Zerek and Derek.

"A giant fluffy pink elephant!" said Billy. "I mean, honestly!"

"Yes," said Zerek irritably. "You're meant to blend in with your surroundings when you morph."

"I was trying to turn myself into a watering can," Derek explained sheepishly. "But it all went a bit wrong—"

"You get everything wrong!" snapped Kerek.

"I don't know why the Great Computer insisted on us bringing him along in the first place," said Zerek. "He's been nothing but trouble from the moment we—"

"For heaven's sake, shut up!" Billy shouted. "All of you!"

"Dear, dear," said Kevin the hamster. "Who rattled *his* cage?"

Billy sighed. Not only could Derek never morph into anything sensible, but he'd also taught Billy's pet hamster to talk. Now it was difficult to persuade Kevin to be quiet. Billy might have known that he would stick his oar in.

"Yeah, who ruffled his fur?" said Kevin the hamster, turning to Kevin the hamster. "That's what I want to know."

"Search me," said a third Kevin the hamster. "Do *you* know why he's in such a bad mood?"

"No idea," said the fourth Kevin the hamster. "He was born grumpy if you ask me."

"Hang on a minute," Billy muttered. He jumped off the bed, rushed over to the cage and peered in. "Oh, what?" he exclaimed.

Kevin was reclining on a soft bed of crumpled tissue paper, surrounded by three other hamsters, identical to him

in every way. One of them was grooming his fur. One was polishing his nails. A third was delicately peeling him a grape.

"This is the life," he sighed.

"What on earth's going on?" Billy demanded. "When I went downstairs there was just one of you."

"They're my three little helpers," said Kevin. "Aren't you?"

The three attendant hamsters nodded solemnly.

Billy spun round and glared at Derek. "You've been using that Megawotsit Multi-Thingy Gizmo of yours again, haven't you?"

Derek shrugged. "Might have," he said. "But there's no harm done," he added. "And anyway, Kevin asked me to. Insisted! Said he was lonely; said he needed a bit of company."

"But how could you?" said Billy.

"Oh, it was easy," said Derek. "I just pressed the button and—"

"That's not what I mean!" Billy interrupted him. "The last time you used it I found forty-six Silases in the bedroom. And what a mess that was!"

"That was a mistake," said Derek. "It's working perfectly now – and all you have to do to reverse it is press this button here." He pointed the gizmo at the cage and pressed three times.

Zap. Zap. Zap.

Kevin's three helpers disappeared.

"Oi!" shouted Kevin the hamster indignantly. "I was enjoying that!"

"Well, I'm sorry, Kevin," said Billy, "but you'll just have to peel your own grapes!"

"But it's not fair!" Kevin complained.

"Life's not fair!" said Billy grumpily. "I've got to deliver Mrs Turbot's leaflets, wash Mr Arkwright's car, mow Mrs Ramsden's lawn – *and* tidy up the mess in here!"

Kerek stepped forwards. "It sounds like *you* could do with a little helper," he said.

"No!" said Billy.

"All your chores would be done for you," said Zerek.

"No," said Billy. "Absolutely not."

"But it's as easy as cake," said Derek. "And you've just seen how simple it is to reverse it."

"All the same," said Billy, a little less certainly.

"You'll have time to put your feet up," said Kerek, "and—"

"And go and play on my friend Simon's computer game," said Billy. "Hmmm. When you put it like that . . ." He nodded. "OK, then. But nothing had better go wrong."

"Nothing will," said Kerek.

"Have a little faith," said Zerek.

Derek raised the gizmo and pointed it at Billy.

Billy swallowed. "Why have I got the horrible feeling that I'm going to live to regret this," he muttered.

Derek pressed the button. There was a dazzling flash of light and an odd *boing*! "Hmm, it's never done that before," said Derek. "Still, never mind."

Chapter Two

Billy crept down the stairs, along the hall and out through the front door. The catch clicked softly in the lock.

Mr Barnes frowned. He looked at his wife. "Was that Billy going out?" he said. "I distinctly told him that he couldn't go round to Simon's." He jumped up from the table, strode crossly into the hall and shouted upstairs.

"Billy? Billy, are you up there?"

Billy appeared at the top of the

stairs and beamed down at him vacantly. "Yes, Father?" he said.

"I . . . errm. Nothing, Billy. Just . . . I could have sworn . . ." He nodded seriously. "How's that bedroom coming along? I hope it's looking a bit tidier."

Billy giggled. "As tidy as a tadpole," he said.

Mr Barnes sighed. "Stop being silly,

Billy." He pulled Mrs Turbot's box of school-fair leaflets out from under the stairs and picked it up. "Just go and deliver these leaflets."

Billy nodded and marched down the stairs. "Your wish is my umbrella," he announced as he slipped the box under his arm and headed for the front door.

"And try not to take all day!"

"As quick as a panda – and twice as smelly. That's me!" said Billy brightly.

Mr Barnes frowned. "And when you've done the leaflets, there's Mr Arkwright's car and Mrs Ramsden's lawn," he said. "Don't forget!"

Billy opened the door.

"And don't slam the—"

SLAM!

Mr Barnes returned to the kitchen. "Was it my imagination?" he said to his wife, "or was Billy behaving even more strangely than usual?"

At the first door he came to, Billy stopped, removed a leaflet from the box and neatly tore it in half. Then in half again. And again, and again, and again . . .

"Greetings, porcupines!" he cried out as he tossed the handful of

confetti into the air. "And may your vegetables all explode with joy!'

It was the same story at the next house. And the one after that. And the one after that. Both sides of the road, he did; four roads in all, until all the leaflets were gone. Then, chortling happily, he placed the empty box on his head.

"My herrings have wings," he trilled as he skipped off to carry out his second chore.

Mr Arkwright's dirty blue car was parked in the drive next to the house. There was a note under the windscreen.

Dear Billy, it said. *Thank you for coming! You'll find everything you need in the kitchen.* And it was signed. *W. W. Arkwright.*

21

Billy made his way round to the back of the house. There was a bucket and sponge on the mat. There was a bottle of tomato ketchup on the shelf, a can of whipped cream by the fridge, a packet of Rich Tea biscuits beside the kettle. Billy took them all. He marched back to the car.

"My gravy is lumpy and my custard is blue," Billy sang tunelessly as he dolloped the ketchup and squirted the foaming whipped cream all over the car and rubbed it around with the sponge.

Then, ripping open the packet of Rich Tea, Billy pulled out two biscuits at a time, scrunched them up in his hands and tossed them at the car. Handful after handful, he threw – at the windscreen, the headlamps, the hubcaps.

"Ooh, doctor, is that a grapefruit behind your ear?" he chirruped happily. "Ding-dong! The frogs go bong! May-day, may-day!"

Finally, he stood back, folded his arms and looked at the car admiringly.

"Frib-frib!" he exclaimed and dashed off to complete his final chore.

"Ah, Billy," said Mrs Ramsden when

Billy's grinning face appeared at her kitchen window. "Have you come to do my lawn for me? You are a good boy."

She dried her hands on the tea towel and bustled outside.

"Did you know you've got a cardboard box on your head, dear?" she said.

"Avast there, me hearties!" Billy cried and covered one eye with his hand as a pretend eyepatch.

"Oh, I see," said Mrs Ramsden, smiling uncertainly. "I've got a pirate to mow my lawn for me today, have I?" She opened the shed and pulled out the rotary mower. "You've used it before, so you know what to do," she said. "But remember, always keep the flex behind you."

Billy nodded. "Your hula hoop is my

command," he muttered gleefully.

Mrs Ramsden frowned. "There we are then, dear," she said as she plugged it in. "I'll go and see about a nice glass of iced lemonade."

Billy chuckled happily as he flicked the switch. The lawnmower whirred into action.

"Mountains of yoghurt and oceans of jam," he cried out as he swept the mower through the long grass cutting first one wide arc, then a second, and then a long line between the two, until the first of three letters appeared.

B

"Come on in, the baked beans are lovely!" Billy yodelled, as a long sweeping curve of the mower resulted in the second letter.

U

"A turnip has kidnapped my tortoise!"

Up and down, he mowed. Up and down. The third letter appeared.

M

Chapter Three

It was four o'clock when Billy made his way home. He hadn't enjoyed Simon's new game that much. It wasn't a patch on the original *Splat Attack*.

As he turned into Beech Avenue, he noticed the thick sprinkling of confetti all over the doormat of number 2.

"Odd," thought Billy.

When he saw a similar pile at number 4, he frowned. At number 6, he paused and scratched his head. At number 8, he could hide his curiosity no longer. He walked up the path, crouched and picked up one of the scraps of paper. There was printed writing on one side.

SCHOOL FA— it said.

"Uh-oh!" Billy groaned.

Quickening his step, Billy hurried along towards number 32, where he lived. Each house he passed had the same pile of confetti on its doorstep, while more of the stuff was blowing out from the gardens opposite.

"Oh, no," he groaned. He was beginning to panic now.

Then he saw a car – the blue car that Mr Arkwright was so proud of. It wasn't blue now. It was red and white, covered in a thick dripping gloop and studded with biscuit crumbs.

Billy froze. His jaw dropped. His

heart pounded. Things were even worse than he'd imagined.

Running now, he hurried home and dashed round the back of the house. Then, scarcely daring to look, he pulled himself up on the fence and peered over into Mrs Ramsden's garden. He saw the three huge letters mown into the long grass.

"Oh my goodness!" he exclaimed.

Billy raced upstairs and burst into his bedroom. A fluffy elephant, a rubber ring and a beach ball looked up calmly.

"We knew it was you," said Kerek. "You're *so* noisy."

"What on earth's been going on?" Billy shouted.

"Well," said Derek, smiling. "Zerek's been showing me something clever you can do with an elephant and a rubber ring, and—"

"And how many times do I have to tell you?" said Zerek impatiently. "It won't work if you bend your trunk!"

Billy shook his head impatiently. "I don't mean you lot," he said. "What's Billy been up to?"

There was silence as the blobby toys morphed back into Blobheads.

Kerek frowned. "I thought you were going to play with that friend of yours, what's his name?"

"Susan," said Derek.

"Simon," said Billy. "But I don't mean me-Billy. I mean the other one. The other Billy."

"Oh, him!" said Zerek. "He's out doing your chores."

"Doing chores?" said Billy. "He's gone mad!"

"What, madder than you?" said Kevin the hamster. "That's hard to imagine."

"He's torn every single one of Mrs Turbot's leaflets into a hundred pieces," Billy said. "He's covered Mr Arkwright's car with ketchup and broken biscuits. And you wouldn't believe what he's done to Mrs Ramsden's lawn!"

Kerek, Zerek and Derek huddled together. Their pulsing red and purple blobs fizzed and buzzed.

"Curious," said Kerek at last.

"Very odd," said Zerek.

"What?" said Billy.

Derek pulled the gizmo from his belt and inspected it closely. "I'm sure I didn't break the wizzometer. Perhaps the jambles are a bit dirty."

"It's more likely to be a problem with your digital loops," said Kerek.

"Unless your oscillating flange is on the blink," said Zerek.

Kerek took the small black box from Derek and shook it. Something rattled inside. "Then again," he said, "with this model, replication is never going to be an exact science."

"Not an exact science!" Billy exclaimed loudly.

"Is that you, Billy?" a voice floated up from downstairs. It was Mr Barnes.

"Yes, Dad," Billy called back.

"You're back earlier than I thought. Dinner'll be about another half hour. Sausage and syrup casserole, and chocolate-chip onion ice cream for afters. I expect you're hungry."

Billy groaned. The smell of meat and toffee floated up the stairs. "Not *that* hungry, Dad," he said, wishing for the thousandth time that his gourmet dad would simply open a box of fish fingers for a change.

"You will be," said his dad confidently. "Anyway, better get back to my sauce. And thanks again for taking Silas to the park. I hope you both had fun."

Billy's bedroom fell completely still as Mr Barnes's words sank in. Billy looked at the Blobheads. The Blobheads looked at one another.

"Oh, no," said Billy.

"Oh, no," said the Blobheads.

"Oh, yes!" said Kevin the hamster.

"You don't think?" said Kerek, pulling the Great Computer from his belt and stabbing at the buttons.

"Not with Silas," said Derek, his blobby head wobbling with distress.

"*Waaaaaah!*" screamed Zerek. His purple and red blobs flashed on and off. "Purple alert! Purple alert!" he shrieked. "Don't panic! Mad, crazy, silly Billy has abducted the High Emperor of the Universe. *Waaaaaaah!*"

"Control yourself, Zerek!" Kerek commanded.

"Yes, pull yourself to pieces," said Derek.

"Together!" Billy corrected him.

"Pull yourself to pieces!" all three Blobheads chanted in unison.

"Our first duty is to maintain the safety of the Most High Emperor of the Universe," said Kerek.

"We have been neglectful in that duty," said Zerek. "Now we must make amends. We must find this silly Billy and zap him back to whence he came."

"Blobheads to the rescue!" Derek cried.

Chapter Four

Billy never liked going out with the Blobheads, but on this occasion even he could see that there was no choice. His baby brother was in the clutches of a loony version of himself – a Billy so silly it had already messed up all the chores it had been given. What would it do with Silas? Smear *him* all over with tomato ketchup? Tear *him* into tiny little pieces? Give him a haircut? It didn't bear thinking about.

"Are you ready?" he asked the Blobheads.

"Ready and willing," said the red and purple blobby skateboard.

"Is that you, Kerek?" said Billy.

"It is," said the skateboard. "Zerek's the jacket."

"As always," the blobby jacket complained. "I don't know why I always have to be. I'd far rather be something with wheels . . ."

"Guess who!" said the helmet. "It's me. Derek."

Billy looked at the heavy metal Viking helmet with curved and pointed horns. "I'd never have guessed," he muttered. "Come on, then. Let's go."

With the jacket over his shoulder, the helmet on his head and the skateboard under his arm, Billy made for the door.

"Wait a minute," said Kerek. "Where's the gizmo?"

"I thought you had it," said Zerek. "Derek?"

Derek shook his blobby head. "I haven't got it," he said.

"Well someone must have!" said Billy. "It can't just have disappeared." He frowned. "Can it?"

There was a jangle and rattle as a tiny paw tried to pull the black gizmo in through the bars of the cage.

"Kevin!" shouted Billy. "What are you doing with that?"

"I wanted my little helpers back," said Kevin the hamster.

"Give it to me at once!" said Billy.

"Ask nicely."

Billy snatched it away and dashed off. The bedroom door slammed.

"Charming!" said Kevin huffily.

40

Billy was at the top of the stairs when the knock came on the front door. He hesitated. Mr Barnes emerged from the kitchen and opened it.

"Look at this!" came an angry voice. It was Mrs Turbot. She let a handful of the confetti flutter down on to the carpet. "My leaflets!" she said. "He's done this to each and every one of them."

"Uh-oh," Billy muttered.

"Just go!" said the skateboard urgently.

"All right," said Billy. He raced down the stairs.

"There he is!" said Mrs Turbot.

Mr Barnes turned. "Slow down a minute, young man," he said. Billy ran past him. "Billy, I want a word with you—"

"Sorry, Dad, Mrs Turbot," said Billy

hurriedly. "Can't stop. It's a matter of life and death."

And with that, he leaped down the steps and on to the garden path. Mr Arkwright appeared at the other end. His face was purple with rage.

"What on earth do you think you've been playing at?" he roared.

"Is there a problem?" Mr Barnes called. "Didn't Billy clean your car properly?"

"Clean it properly?" Mr Arkwright blustered. "He's turned it into a giant trifle!"

"A what?" said Mr Barnes.

"I can explain," said Billy. He dropped the skateboard on to the path and jumped on. "But not now," he said, as he sped past Mr Arkwright and out on to the pavement.

Mrs Ramsden's head appeared

above the fence. She looked troubled. "I know I should be grateful for the extra help," she said. "But . . . but . . ." She burst into tears. "There's an enormous B-U-M on my lawn!'

"Whoooah!" Billy exclaimed and flapped his arms about wildly as the skateboard hurtled across the road, skidded round the corner and flew through the park gates. It was half-past six and, apart from an old man walking his whippet, the park was deserted.

"Where are they?" Billy asked, his heart thumping wildly. "Where have they gone?"

He jumped from the skateboard, picked it up and ran across the grass in the direction of the playground. There was no one playing football on the pitches he crossed, no one playing tennis on the courts he passed – and as he approached the playground, that too looked empty.

The swings were hanging motionless; the roundabout was still. Then a voice broke the silence.

"Rejoice! Rejoice! My budgie lies over the ocean and the gerbils are all running free!"

"There!" screamed the skateboard.

"At the top of the slide!" yelled the jacket.

Billy looked up. And there, seated at the very top with his legs on the steps and a cardboard box on his head, was the spitting image of himself. It was like looking in a mirror – apart, of course, from the cardboard box.

The other Billy waved. "Waiter, waiter, there's a hippopotamus in my soup!" he cried.

"Where's my baby brother, Silas?" Billy shouted up.

His double looked down and grinned. "My bubble and squeak is burned to a crisp!" he announced happily.

"This is hopeless," said Billy. "I'm coming up there."

Taking the steps two at a time, Billy bounded up to the top of the slide. As he arrived, the other Billy pushed himself off.

"Wheeee!" he cried. "The boats are full of treacle!"

Billy watched him sliding down and landing on the ground with a bump. His baby brother was not with him.

"Silas!" he shouted, scanning all round the park. "*Silas*!"

"Blobber-blobber, goo!" came a tiny voice from behind him.

Billy spun round and looked down. And there was Silas, sitting in the sandpit, waving his spade in the air.

"Silas!" Billy exclaimed.

"High Emperor of the Universe!" shouted the jacket.

"Thank Blob!" muttered the helmet.

Billy flew down the slide, dashed to the sandpit and picked Silas up in his arms. "Oh, Silas," he gasped. "You're safe now!"

"Blobberlob!" Silas gurgled.

"Yes, it's me," said Billy, hugging him tightly.

Silas twisted round and pointed a podgy finger at the figure with the

cardboard box on his head now sitting at one end of the see-saw.

"One hump or two?" it was shouting.

"Billa-blobber-lob!" said Silas and giggled.

"No, Silas," said Billy. "*I'm* the real Billy. That's . . . that's Silly Billy."

Silas's face creased up into a smile. "Blibby-slibby."

"But not for much longer," the skateboard announced. "Billy, zap the impostor!"

Billy nodded and placed Silas gently on the ground. He raised the gizmo. He lined up his double in the sights. Then, with a trembling finger, he pressed the button.

ZAP!

There was a loud bang and a blinding flash and . . .

"OH, NO!" Billy screamed.

The playground was suddenly full. There were three boys on each of the swings, a dozen on the slide, twenty on the roundabout, countless more in the sandpit, on the field, up the trees – and every one a copy, not of Billy – but of Silly Billy. The noise was deafening.

"My piano is in need of a cheese and pickle sandwich!" cried one.

"You must take two rhinos four times a day," cried another.

And a chorus of "Purple pie! Purple pie! We want purple pie!" echoed from the sandpit.

"You pressed the wrong button!" the helmet shouted.

"I didn't," Billy shouted back. "The gizmo must have malfunctioned."

"My nose is a tulip. My nose is a tulip."

"The doughnuts are wearing silk pyjamas!"

"But only when there's an eel in the month—"

"DO SOMETHING!" Billy roared.

Without saying a word, the skateboard morphed back into Kerek. He grabbed the gizmo and stabbed frantically at the buttons.

"You're right," he muttered. "It has malfunctioned. I think the nether-sprockets might be broken." He opened the back, pulled a buzzing screwdriver from his belt and poked about inside.

All around him, the multitude of Silly Billies were running amok, jumping, jostling and gurgling with joy.

"My parrots are inconvenient!"

"Saddle up the poodle!"

"Tickle the walrus!"

"Hurry *up*!" said Billy urgently. His countless doubles were getting increasingly overexcited.

"Nearly done," said Kerek. He clicked the back of the gizmo shut. "Everyone *not* a Silly Billy get behind me, now!" he bellowed.

Billy grabbed Silas, held him in his arms and ran back. He checked that he was still wearing the jacket and helmet. "Ready," he said.

"Right," said Kerek grimly. He raised the gizmo and set the co-ordinates to wide-angle. The tip of his tentacle hovered over the button. "Here goes," he muttered.

ZAP!

There was a bang and a flash – louder and more blinding than before. And then silence.

The silly Billies had vanished, each and every one. The empty swings swung. The empty roundabout ground to a halt.

"Phew!" said Billy.

Silas turned to Billy and hugged him. "Blibba-slibba blobbel!" he cooed.

Chapter Five

Billy was in trouble. Big trouble. Even after he'd delivered Mrs Turbot's leaflets – in one piece this time – and cleaned up all the scraps of paper his double had dropped. Even after he'd washed the gloop off Mr Arkwright's car and polished it till it gleamed. Even after he'd mown Mrs Ramsden's lawn properly . . .

"Never in all my born days," Mr Barnes told him, "have I witnessed such naughty behaviour!"

Billy hung his head. It was pointless trying to explain what had really happened. And anyway, it had been stupid of him to trust the Blobheads. He sighed. Perhaps that was why his double had turned out to be a Silly Billy in the first place.

"You'll be getting no pocket money for the next six weeks," Mr Barnes said.

Billy nodded glumly.

"Not that you'll need it," he went on, "because you're also grounded."

Billy sighed again. It would mean spending more time than ever with the blobby aliens and his talking hamster.

"And if you thought that by carrying out your chores so badly you'd avoid them in future, then you were very much mistaken," his father was saying. "From now on you will help with the washing up, you will vacuum the carpets and wash the kitchen floor every other day. Now go to your room."

Billy turned to go.

"Oh, and another thing," Mr Barnes said. "From now on, you can get your own breakfast."

Billy tried not to smile. *Every cloud*

has a silver lining, he thought as he headed up the stairs. That morning, Mr Barnes had started the day with a kipper and strawberry jam soufflé. Billy would enjoy cornflakes for a change.

"Oh, it's you," said a voice as Billy walked into his bedroom, and the long fluffy purple and red snake in the middle of the floor morphed into Derek.

The inflatable blobby armchair and the doll's house turned back into Kerek and Zerek.

Billy stared at the three Blobheads furiously. "You imbeciles!" he roared.

"Shhh!" hissed Zerek. "I don't want you waking Silas. The High Emperor of the Universe has had a very trying day."

"*He's* had a trying day!" said Billy. "What about me? You've made things worse than ever! Now, instead of three chores to do, I've got dozens."

Derek smiled eagerly. "I can make you as many helpers as you like," he said. "Now that the gizmo's working properly again."

Billy shook his head in disbelief. "Don't you lot ever learn?" he said.

"There isn't much for hyper-intelligent beings like ourselves *to* learn," said Kerek.

"Right!" Billy snorted. He turned on Derek. "Give me the gizmo. I'm confiscating it."

"I can't," said Derek.

"Come on," Billy persisted. "I know you too well. You'll be using it again the moment my back's turned."

"I won't," said Derek, his blobby head growing redder than usual.

"De-rek!" said Billy, holding out his hand.

Derek hung his head. "I can't find it," he said.

Billy's eyes widened in horror. "Can't find it?" he said. "Are you sure?"

Derek nodded.

"Well, *I* haven't got it," said Kerek.

"Neither have I," said Zerek.

"Where did you lose it?" said Billy. "In the park? On the street?"

"If I knew where I'd lost it then I'd go and find it again," Derek wailed miserably.

"But what if someone else finds it?" said Billy. "What if they play with it. If they press its buttons . . ." He sat down on the corner of the bed and held his head in his hands. "Oh, good grief," he groaned. "This is awful."

"Never mind, Billy," said Kerek, patting him on his shaking shoulders. "It could be worse!"

Billy looked up wearily. "How?" he said.

ZAP! Bang! Flash!

"Yes!" shouted Kevin the hamster triumphantly. "My helpers . . . *fffpllppffllppff*! Waaah! HELP!"

All eyes turned to the cage in the corner. Fur was sticking out from between every bar, as if a great animal had been stuffed inside. It wasn't one animal though. It was many. Dozens and dozens of identical talking hamsters all crammed together in Kevin's cage. And at the top of the pile, the real Kevin himself – the missing gizmo clutched in his trembling paws.

"Hyper-intelligent beings, I *don't* think!" he squeaked indignantly at the three Blobheads. "I thought you said this thing was working properly now!"

Billy sighed. "And you *believed* them!"

BLOBHEADS titles available
from Macmillan

Read all about the Blobheads' adventures!

1. Invasion of the Blobs	0 330 38972 6	£2.99
2. Talking Toasters	0 330 38973 4	£2.99
3. School Stinks!	0 330 38974 2	£2.99
4. Beware of the Babysitter	0 330 38975 0	£2.99
5. Garglejuice	0 330 38976 9	£2.99
6. Silly Billy	0 330 38977 7	£2.99

All Macmillan titles can be ordered at your local bookshop
or are available by post from:

Book Service by Post
PO Box 29, Douglas, Isle of Man IM99 1BQ

Credit cards accepted. For details:
Telephone: 01624 675137
Fax: 01624 670923
E-mail: bookshop@enterprise.net

Free postage and packing in the UK.
Overseas customers: add £1 per book (paperback)
and £3 per book (hardback).

The prices shown below are correct at the time of going to press.
However, Macmillan Publishers reserve the right to show new retail
prices on covers which may differ from those previously advertised.